D0466927

How Zinnia Got Her Name

Based on the Original Flower Fairies™ Books
by Cicely Mary Barker

Frederick Warne

In Flower Fairyland, every
fairy has a flower and
every flower has a fairy.

All the fairies except one. And because she doesn't have a flower, she doesn't have a name. "If I don't find a flower soon," the little fairy says sadly, "I will have to leave Flower Fairyland."

Sweet Chestnut, a kind-hearted Flower Fairy,
overhears the little fairy crying and takes
pity on her. He throws her a chestnut with
a note inside. "Catch this, little
fairy," he shouts.

To be a Flower Fairy you must:

1. Learn to dance

2. Learn to sew fairy costumes out of petals

3. Learn to look after plants
and flowers

"When you have learnt these lessons, Wild Rose –
the oldest and wisest of the Flower Fairies – will
present you with a flower," Sweet Chestnut adds.

The little fairy whizzes over to where Columbine lives. Columbine is teaching a friend to dance.

The little fairy doesn't want to disturb them, so she hides in the tall grass, learning all the steps by heart.

Next stop is Tansy. She is
the best seamstress in all
of Flower Fairyland.
Tansy is sewing a yellow
dress made out of petals.

The little fairy watches her intently, and she soon knows all the little stitches Tansy uses.

Next the little fairy learns
the most important lesson
of all – how to look after
her plant!

Shirley Poppy is expert at
sowing her seeds far and wide.

Sister Pink is in charge of
trimming her flower's petals
and brother Pink is in
charge of the leaves
and stalks.

That night the little fairy
writes in her diary:

Dear Diary,
Today I learned how
to dance by watching
Columbine practising.
I learned how to sew
Flower Fairy
costumes
from Tansy.

And Poppy,
along with brother
and sister Pink, taught me
how to care for a plant.
I have learnt all of the Flower
Fairy lessons and tomorrow
I will ask Wild Rose if I can
have a flower of my own...

19

The next day,
Wild Rose decides the little
fairy is ready. "Your magical
flower name is... Zinnia!"
she announces.

Zinnia is thrilled to have
a flower of her own.
"At last!" she says. "Now
I have a home in Flower
Fairyland!"

FREDERICK WARNE

Published by the Penguin Group
Penguin Books Ltd, 80 Strand, London WC2R 0RL, England
New York, Australia, Canada, India, New Zealand, South Africa

This edition first published by Frederick Warne 2006
1 3 5 7 9 10 8 6 4 2

ISBN 0 7232 5358 7

Printed in China